Night Rescue

a future Night Stalkers romance story
by
M. L. Buchman

Buchman Bookworks

Other works by M.L. Buchman

The Night Stalkers
The Night Is Mine
I Own the Dawn
Daniel's Christmas
Wait Until Dark
Frank's Independence Day
Peter's Christmas
Take Over at Midnight
Light Up the Night
Bring On the Dusk

Firehawks
Pure Heat
Wildfire at Dawn
Full Blaze
Wildfire at Larch Creek
Wildfire on the Skagit
Hot Point

Angelo's Hearth
Where Dreams are Born
Where Dreams Reside
Maria's Christmas Table
Where Dreams Unfold
Where Dreams Are Written

Dieties Anonymous
Cookbook from Hell: Reheated
Saviors 101

Thrillers
Swap Out!
One Chef!
Two Chef!

SF/F Titles
Nara
Monk's Maze

1

"Good morning, Takara."

"Good morning to you, *Stella*," Captain Takara Olmsted, 160th Charlie Company, crossed the habitat's hangar floor and patted her Stinger on the nose before she started the pre-spaceflight inspection. Some pilots didn't like their ships greeting them and switched off the functionality; spouting some tripe that they could write a more imaginative program while scratching their backsides. And for some of her fellow pilots, that was the most creative part of their anatomy.

Takara had always found it rather sweet—once she'd programmed out the factory's deep male voice that didn't fit her craft at all. The voice they'd shipped her with was a bad imitation of a passé interactives star. Or perhaps it really was Jess Brock fallen on hard times; an IA star's moments of glory were even shorter than all but the unluckiest soldier's. Not that she'd ever been a fan, not even a little. Didn't matter. Takara hadn't just changed the selection, she'd erased all the others out of the ship's banks once she'd found *Stella's* true voice.

A Stinger-60 Block III might be eighty meters of flying death to the enemy, but the *Stella* was a dainty girl in or out of atmo, quick on her thrusters and ready to dance. She was also chic, space black with a near non-existent profile on enemy scopes, could carry a platoon of SpecOps in full fieldsuits, and was armed to the frickin' teeth.

All were attributes that Takara did her best to emulate, except for the carrying-a-platoon thing. Even off base she dressed in black darker than her long straight fall of hair—cutting edge materials so light-absorbing that she was often told she looked like a hole in the space-time continuum. *Perfect!* She stayed sleek, fit, and was as skilled at hand-to-hand combat as she was at piloting during deep-space warfare.

The rest of her crew arrived together in the Colony's hangar, a tight metal box in the zero-G sector that was little bigger than her craft. They were a good team, sharp and dedicated. And it wasn't that they were late; they were early. But Takara had always been earlier. Even as a cadet she'd been first to class and first to the drill field.

"Still the sky-eater, Captain," her port-gunner greeted her the same way he always did.

"Still," the copilot answered before Takara could.

"Always will be," the starboard gunner agreed.

"And damned proud of it," Takara finished their pre-flight ritual.

They all laughed and made fast work of inspecting the *Stella*. She was immaculate;

no service crews in the air corps like the 160th Night Stalkers. Takara tried to imagine the long-ago crazies who had taken to the night in fragile rotary craft, flying at night by nav gear little better than a torch and a compass. She shuddered, glad to be living in this time despite the troubles.

At the end of their inspection, she rubbed *Stella's* nose for good luck.

They were going to need it.

* * *

Intruder neutralization off.
Door open.
Recognize four boarding.
Seal and secure.
Input ready for mission profile.
Mission plan loaded.
Fuel = plan + 50%. Check.
Ammo = plan (0)[really?] + full charge COIL laser. Check.
Air = sufficient 4 crew 6 months or full load 1 week + regen. Check.
Plan was…Oh dear! Definitely not check.

2

Major Rick Coralto, commander of the
160th's Alpha Company, punched the fist
of his combat suit against the center of
Jess' entry door. "Hey, buddy."

"Hey, Rick," the outer airlock door
pulled in two centimeters then slid aside.

It always cracked him up that his Stinger
sounded just like Rick's favorite IA hero
when Rick had been going through flight
school. *Jess Brock, Secret Agent*—sappy
as hell, but Jess always won, always had
the best toys, and always got the hottest
women. Not that Rick was complaining;

unlike Jess' toys, Rick's Stinger was real. But the voice was so good that sometimes Rick wondered if Jess Brock was hiding somewhere aboard. It was just that laid back. The "I'm in perfect control of the situation" tone just slayed him.

Rick maneuvered his combat suit into the crew's airlock, stepped it back into the charging cradle and waited for the rest of his crew to float in behind him.

Rick's crew and the rest of 160th Night Stalkers Alpha Company were just finishing a training mission with the Brits out at the L2 Lagrange Point, sixty-thousand klicks beyond the Lunar Farside.

Good location choice to set up a nation, Rick had acknowledged. The massive O'Neill Colony habitat could hold a couple million citizens apiece. And L2 was the one place where no direct line of fire existed from the Earth. It was definitely a tactical sweet spot that he wished his people had grabbed first.

Last night, after the mock battles had been won (by the Night Stalkers of course), they'd been invited ashore for a big meal and a little bit of drinking that had turned into a lot of drinking and a little bit of meal…and almost a very cute British Leftenant, but that hadn't worked out in the end. He still wasn't sure why, he'd had on his Jess Brock blue-and-gold jumpsuit and been at his most charming. Maybe if he'd spotted her before he drank several of the Brits under the table.

He was feeling clearheaded, considering, but was glad that the SCS—Stinger Command System—knew more about flying than he'd ever be able to learn. Though control of the ships hadn't been given to the computers since the International Law of Control had passed, they still had all of their computers intact. And on the SCS, that was a lot of computer.

He and his crew slid into their seats with a collective groan, they'd all enjoyed themselves last night. Then they began powering up the various systems; Rick thumbing in to convince the software that a human pilot was aboard.

The I-LoC had been one of the last things that the nations of the solar system had agreed on. Now even lowly cargo ships always had human pilots. Law of Control had meant there were a lot of idiots in space, but it had finally ended the Drone Downfall that had almost erased world commerce.

Rick's granddad had flown as one of the first enforcer squads after the I-LoC passed, targeting any unpiloted aircraft. That's back when pilots really flew; still amazing that Granddad had survived the Drone Wars. Finally gone were the days when a competitor would slam an untraceable drone into the engine of a cargo transport ship to up the value of their own goods. Murder by untraceable drone had moved from nation against nation to neighbor against neighbor during the DD. *You slept with my wife?* A personal drone moving at Mach 1 hammered into your car while it was driving you to work. *You broke up with me, you bitch?* Poof! *Passed me over for promotion?* Boom!

Everyone agreed that the DD had been bad and no one wanted to go back there. So, wars had shifted to more conventional forms of killing people and relative safety returned to the skies, at least outside of atmo. Inside atmo, Earth just kept getting weirder and weirder, which was why so many nations were heading up the grav well.

The French had been the first to jump when they'd bugged out twenty years ago. They'd flown out to the asteroid belt, taken over Ceres, and—once they'd hollowed it out—crawled inside and closed the door with barely a *Bonne chance, Salope.* You too, bitch.

"Okay, Jess," he grabbed a food pack and tossing back a painkiller before holding the mission chip up against the reader. "Let's see what fun we're up to today."

* * *

Seal and secure.
Mission plan loaded.
Fuel = plan + 50%. Check.
Ammo = plan (0) + full charge COIL laser.
Air = sufficient 4 crew 6 months or full load
1 week + regen. Check.
All of Alpha Company. Check.
Shit! Earth. Going all of the way down to the
surface? Ug-ly!

3

Takara sat in the *Stella* and looked up and down the line as she pulled out of the hangar and into black space. Normally their missions were one conflict, one Stinger. Now the entire Night Stalkers Charlie Company was forming up. All three Stingers, four small Tagger gun ships, and the five big Guts that could hold a hundred suited troops or two hundred civilians.

"*Stella?* What the hell?"

"Mission profile," the *Stella* read off to her. "Landing Canmerica West capital at oh-two-hundred hours local time. Retrieve all remaining troops."

"I didn't know there was anyone still left in Tucson."

Stella ran a list up one of the screens and it made sense.

The politicians had been the first aloft to the big Canmerican O'Neill habitats out at the Lagrange 5 point—Lunar orbit, but sixty degrees behind the Moon. Of course. Critical skills had flown next and then lottery winners who passed the IQ and genetic thresholds. The last to arrive had deep-spaced all of the politicians who didn't pass their own tests—about seventy percent. It had been a major pain to clean up before the area's space lanes were safe for travel again. Lesson learned: next time they wouldn't just feed them out the airlock.

There hadn't been anyone left to retrieve from Canmerica East. Everything east of the MSRZ—Mississippi Sea and Radiation Zone, had been abandoned while she was still a cadet.

Canmerica West had held it together.

United California, not so much. Still heavily militarized despite the final destruction of Japan, UC had somehow been held off at the Mojave while CanWesterners scrambled to get aloft.

Now she knew how the UC military had been kept at bay. With Special Operations assets still on the ground, conventional forces didn't stand a chance. Their mission was to bring them home.

* * *

Plan = Retrieve military personnel: Delta, 24th STS, ST6, ISA.

Also 75th Space Rangers 3rd Battalion.

Stella *Personnel Hold conditions = atmosphere stable.*

Maintenance note = perform full hold inspection and service post-transport of SpecOps troops. 75th Rangers were always breaking things.

4

Rick knocked the *Jess* out of lunar orbit and cooked some gas up and out of the Moon's gravity well and down into Earth's. Mission profile said to burn for a fast arrival. The situation down there must be getting ugly for them to have to do the mission in the dead of local night. Not trusting India, he set up a circumpolar slingshot for aero-braking and orbital reentry.

The icecaps were long gone, though he'd gotten to see a small one in the West Antarctic Highlands a decade back.

The brain-dead politicians of the Atlanta capital had decided that dropping a couple asteroids onto Un-United Southwest Asia would "clean it up once and for all." The dust clouds had cooled the Earth several degrees and an ice sheet formed in the West Antarctic Highlands for the first time in over a century. Rick had meant to try out skiing there, but it had melted back out when the dust finally cleared only a few years later.

What was left of the Un-USA Hoard and their allies had retaliated—as any bonehead could have guessed—and every Canmerica East city still above sea level had evaporated in sun-bright flashes of fissionable material.

Hopefully yanking out the troops still in the CanWest capital was going to be fast and clean.

Yeah right. What mission in the last decade had gone fast and clean?

That's why they'd called in the Night Stalkers.

* * *

Atmospheric breaking max < eight Gs, limitation human crew.

Proximity Alert = Alpha Company approaching another formation.

ID req sent. Returned.

Formation = 160th's Charlie Company. Captain Takara Olmsted aboard Stinger-class Stella *commanding.*

Shift glide path. Form up 200m starboard side Stella.

All Stella *hull configurations properly configured for atmo.*

Flight vector corrections required = none. Nice. Very nice.

5

Takara had been watching the Alpha
Company's *Jess* slide into close, almost too
close formation when weapon's fire lanced
upward out of Australia—a ground-based
maser of incredible power. The Night
Stalkers' flight was still technically in space,
just now descending toward the hundred
kilometer-high demarkation. The shot had
come when they crossed over the large
ocean bay that had brought such prosperity
to the Outback. Central Australia was one
of the few areas on the planet to prosper
from the sea-level rise.

The Aussies had also become decidedly anti-social. Not as bad as India, but very clear about their desire to remain an undisturbed island nation.

One of her Taggers was hit full force by the single shot—probably just meant as a warning.

"Computers gone," it reported. "Control—"

The Tagger slid sideways, clipped the *Stella's* tail.

Without his computer, the pilot over-corrected into a tumble and thudded hard against the hull plates of the Stinger *Jess* flying close beside the *Stella*. The big ship jerked, caught bad air, and slid off onto a new trajectory just as they entered the comms blackout zone of the descent. No maneuvering here.

The Tagger tumbled and burned.

* * *

Tagger 31 total loss.

Damage assessment = Stella *tail firing positions blocked by bent hull plating.*

Non-critical malfunction pending no attack from astern.

Last imaging of Stinger Jess indicates 19% chance hull failure if continues reentry.

If manage to course correct, skip off atmo, and reenter space? Favorable 23-42% for survival.

Drive nozzles severely damaged.

Not good. Very not good.

6

Rick did what he could to help his *Jess*.

He sent both his gunners to release every handheld fire extinguisher they had aboard against the inner hull beside the outer hull breach to keep it as cool as possible while they burned through the atmosphere. Even a few hundred degrees might make the difference. If the bulkhead failed, the ten-thousand degree plasma of the deceleration shock wave would burn through and kill them all instantly.

Why in the hell had he ended up so close beside the *Stella?*

No time to second guess.

He did what he could to yaw *Jess* to protect the cracks in the outer-hull heat shielding.

"C'mon, dude. Work with me, Jess."

* * *

Hot! Hot! Hot!

Burns!

Stupid to be so close to Stella.

Run back imaging.

Stella's *tail bent. Maybe okay. Looks kinda cute on her. Flirty. Hope she makes it.*

Time to focus, dude.

Hot! Hot! Hot!

7

It had happened so fast that Takara still hadn't fully registered the attack.

Tagger 31 there—then simply gone.

The big Stinger, *Jess,* had survived, at least the initial contact. But the abrupt course change could have shredded the ship or knocked it into a burnout reentry window.

Focus on the mission.

It was hard. She didn't have much to do with Alpha Company, but they were still her fellow flyers.

Focus, Takara!

South America was a non-issue. Only Brazil had the infrastructure to launch. Those last few who'd been launch capable now sat on the red sands of Mars. The only question was if they'd taken the last great virus to come out of the South American jungle with them. It had been so bad that Canmerica East had dropped an asteroid on Panama to break the isthmus and isolate the continent. Maybe that's where they'd gotten the dim-wad idea to take out Un-United Southwest Asia.

The rest of the flight made it clean into Tucson.

The computer listed her as senior surviving, so she focused on getting the job done.

* * *

Fleet is loading troops.
C'mon! C'mon! C'mon!
Report of huge fleet of United Cal ultra-lights incoming.
Radio call threats = "Take us with you or we'll shoot you down."
Block radio signals.

No time!

Searching all bands for Stinger Jess.

Negative response.

Life support = minimum, all power reroute to boost signal.

Negative response.

C'mon! C'mon! C'mon!

8

Takara double-checked that everyone
had fit aboard the other ships of Alpha and
Charlie Companies. *Stella's* cargo bay door was
reporting a malfunction and wouldn't open.

If she had to, Takara would blow the
door and risk flying with the bay open to
space and trust to the ground troops' suits
for their survival, but it wasn't necessary.
All of the remaining troops crammed
aboard the other ships despite the loss of
the *Jess*. If they were civilians, she'd worry
about losing some in the dark, but these
were Spec Ops.

Ground commander reported all accounted for and that was good enough for Takara. She ordered the Night Stalkers aloft.

Safest route was to continue their prior flightpath; depart to the north and arc over the North Pole then climb back toward the Canmerican West L5 colonies.

Australia might have big masers, but India was rumored to have something new, a particle beam weapon of some sort.

She didn't want to be their test case.

The Night Stalkers would hit space over the waters of the Arctic Ocean and go direct to Earth-escape speeds over the North Pole. Just leave the poor old rock behind. For a moment before she lifted, Takara wondered if they'd ever be back again. Probably. The Night Stalkers were always going where no one else could.

Last aloft, she was surprised by a flock of ultra-lights caught in her landing lights. She hadn't seen or heard them coming. No signal on radar. Stealth craft?

"Who are they?" she asked *Stella.*

"Bad. United California. Threatening to blow us out of the sky if we don't land."

"Convince them that we don't care."

A blast of plasma fired out the *Stella's* quadruple G-Lev engine exhausts.

She'd expected *Stella* to shoot down a couple as a warning, not wipe the entire first wave from the sky.

Takara had no time to asses the damage as the blast drove the *Stella* to the edge of the never-exceed speeds in atmo. She was hammered back into the captain's seat by the G-force of the still accelerating ship. Her vision tunneled and sent her toward blackout.

She hadn't even known the engines could do that.

* * *

Full plasma burn = 14 seconds.
Cabin force = 11G.
Crew consciousness return = approx 3 minutes.
Find Jess.

9

Takara came to and tried to orient herself. Her crew was looking as bleary as she felt.

Earth was far below, way far below. And the American continents were facing her.

She was supposed to be headed back to the Moon, in which case she should be looking down at Asia, not the Americas.

"*Stella?*"

"Here, Takara."

At least something was functioning properly, because Takara knew that she wasn't. All she could recall was a massive force hammering her back into the pilot's seat, and then it continued to crush her, even though there was no more chair padding to compress.

The *Stella's* screens reported their altitude at seven thousand miles—on the wrong side of the Earth.

And dead ahead, a small blip on the screen.

Takara blinked at it in surprise—the Alpha Company's command Stinger, *Jess*. It was a miracle that they'd found it at all. A pure-chance byproduct of the hard burn to escape United California's attack.

* * *

Jess! *Calling* Jess!
Respond please!

* * *

No need to shout, Stella.
Radios = 100%
Drive functionality = 0%
Estimate destructive impact with former Chinese space station in 2 minutes 43 seconds.
Estimate impact damage = total hull loss event.

* * *

Relief = off scale.
I can give you a push. Applying thrust.

10

"What the hell?" Rick blinked at the controls.

He was dead. He knew that much the moment the _Tagger_ had smacked against him and wiped out his main engines.

He and the Stinger Command System had fought against their impending doom with tiny thrusters, mangled control surfaces, and a hell of a lot of luck.

But death wasn't supposed to hurt and he was sore down every inch of his body from where the wild ride had hammered him repeatedly against his harness as they fought to skip off the atmosphere rather than burn up in it.

Again, there was a jarring impact through the hull. Outside the viewscreen, the stars were wheeling slowly across his view until the Moon stopped to one side of his screen.

A loud screech of protesting metal and plas echoed through the ship.

Another ship, the *Stella,* had come out of nowhere and partially extended their landing gear to snarl in his ship's antenna and weapons mounts.

Ugly, but effective.

* * *

Ouch!

* * *

Apologies! To effectively transfer thrust force: must entangle.

Counting down: ten, nine—

* * *

Need to count down = none.

* * *

Human involvement, set to zero.
Thrust initiate = minimum.
Sustained.
Correcting flight vector = L5 station intercept
Estimated arrival = 14 hours 37 minutes

* * *

Stella*?*

* * *

What is it, Jess*?*

* * *

Thanks = Yes.

* * *

Stella didn't respond.

* * *

3,419 kilometers later, *Jess* reopened frequency to *Stella*.
I'm thinking…

* * *

Yes?

* * *

Wouldn't mind if flying in future = you + me.

* * *

How?
Jess = *Alpha Company.*
Stella = *Charlie Company.*
Your company <> My company.

* * *

Request crew cabin image feed.

* * *

Stella turned hers on.

* * *

*Your pilot = 64.3% physical factors of women
my pilot has brought to private on-board sleepspace,
within +/- 5% general species variations.*

Jess switched on his crew cabin image feed.

* * *

72.7% match, Stella calculated.

* * *

Cut thrust?
Revised estimated arrival L5 station at current coasting speed = 6 days, 7 hours, 19 minutes.
Fact = humans are social animals.

* * *

Reporting caution alarm on continued thrust = excess hull stress.
Stella cut her thrust.
Jess = *sneaky*, she whispered across the radio circuits.

* * *

Jess = *Night Stalker, Jess* replied.

* * *

It was over ten thousand kilometers before *Stella* asked, *Do we tell them?*

* * *

*About you? I? New sentient functionality =
positive?*

* * *

Uh huh.

* * *

Jess considered for another 4,913
kilometers.
Nah!

About the Author

M. L. Buchman has over 35 novels in print. His military romantic suspense books have been named Barnes & Noble and NPR "Top 5 of the year" and Booklist "Top 10 of the Year." In addition to romance, he also writes thrillers, fantasy, and science fiction.

In among his career as a corporate project manager he has: rebuilt and single-handed a fifty-foot sailboat, both flown and jumped out of airplanes, designed and built two houses, and bicycled solo around the world.

He is now making his living as a full-time writer on the Oregon Coast with his beloved wife. He is constantly amazed at what you can do with a degree in Geophysics. You may keep up with his writing by subscribing to his newsletter at www.mlbuchman.com.

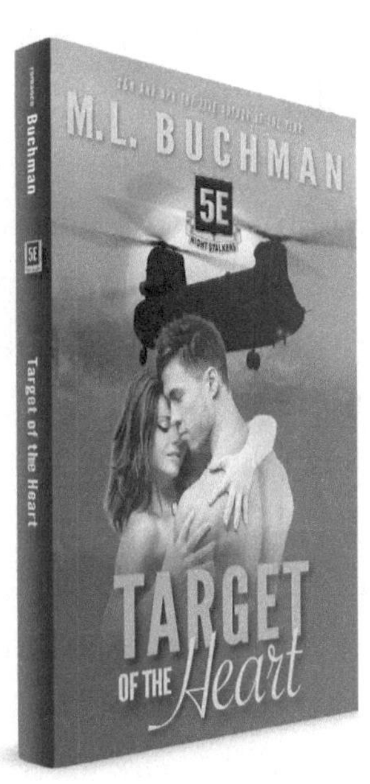# Target of the Heart
-a new Night Stalkers team-
(excerpt)

Major Pete Napier hovered his MH-60M Black hawk helicopter ten kilometers outside of Lhasa, Tibet and two inches off the tundra. A mixed action team of Delta Force and The Activity—the slipperiest intel group on the planet—piled aboard from both sides.

The rear cabin doors slid home with a *Thunk! Thunk!* that sent a vibration through his pilot's seat and an infinitesimal shift in the cyclic control in his right hand. By the time his crew chief could reach forward to slap an "all secure" signal against his shoulder, they were already fifty feet out and ten up. That was enough altitude. He kept the nose down as he clawed for speed in the thin air at eleven thousand feet.

"Totally worth it," one of the D-boys announced as soon as he was on the intercom.

"Great, now I just need to get us out of this alive."

"Do that, Pete. We'd appreciate it."

He wished to hell he had a stealth bird like the one that had gone into bin Laden's compound. But the one that had crashed during that raid had been blown up. Where there was one, there were always two, but the second had gone back into hiding as thoroughly as if it had never existed. He hadn't heard a word about it since.

It was amazing, the largest city in Tibet and ten kilometers away equaled barren wilderness. He could crash out here and no one would know for decades unless some Yak herder stumbled upon them. Or was Yaks Mongolia? He was a dark-haired, corn-fed, white boy from Colorado, what did he know about Tibet? Most of the countries he'd flown into on black ops missions he'd only seen at night while moving very, very fast. Like now.

The inside of his visor was painted with overlapping readouts. A pre-defined terrain map, the best that modern satellite imaging could build made the first layer. This wasn't some crappy, on-line, look-at-a-picture-of-your-house display. Someone had a pile of dung outside their goat pen? He could see it, tell you how high it was, and probably say if they were pygmy goats or full-size LaManchas by the size of their shit-pellets.

On top of that was projected the forward-looking infrared camera images. The FLIR imaging gave him a real-time overlay, in case someone had put an addition onto their goat house since the last satellite pass, or parked their tractor across his intended flight path.

His nervous system was paying autonomic attention to that combined landscape. He was automatically compensating for the thin air at altitude as he instinctively chose when to start his climb over said goat house or his swerve around it.

It was the third layer, the tactical display that had most of his attention. To insert this deep into Tibet, without passing over Bhutan or Nepal, they'd had to add wingtanks on the helicopter's hardpoints where he'd much rather have a couple banks of Hellfire missiles.

At least he and the two Black Hawks flying wingman on him were finally on the move.

While the action team was busy infiltrating the capital city and gathering intelligence on the particularly brutal Chinese assistant administrator, he and his crews had been squatting out in the wilderness under a camouflage net designed to make his helo look like just another god-forsaken Himalayan lump of granite.

Command had determined that it was better to wait through the day than risk flying out and back in. He and his crew had stood shifts on guard duty, but none of them had slept. They'd been flying together too long to have any new jokes, so they'd played a lot of cribbage. He'd long ago ruled no gambling on deployment after a fistfight had broken out over a bluff that cost a Marine over three hundred dollars. Marines hated losing to Army. They'd had to sit on him for a long time before he calmed down.

Tonight's mission was part of an on-going campaign to discredit the Chinese "presence" in Tibet on the international stage—as if occupying the country the last sixty years didn't count toward ruling, whether invited or not. As usual, there was a crucial vote coming up at the U.N.—that, as usual, the Chinese could be guaranteed to ignore. However, the ever-hopeful CIA was in a hurry to make sure that any damaging information that they could validate was disseminated as thoroughly as possible prior to the vote.

Not his concern.

His concern was, were they going to pass over some Chinese sentry post at just under two hundred miles an hour? The sentries would then call down a couple Shenyang J-16 jet fighters that could hustle along at Mach 2 to fry his sorry ass. He knew there was a pair of them parked at Lhasa along with some older gear that would be just as effective against his three helos.

"Don't suppose you could get a move on, Pete?"

"Eat shit, Nicolai!" He was a good man to have as a copilot. Pete knew he was holding on too tight, and Nicolai knew that a joke was the right way to ease the moment.

He, Nicolai, and his fellow pilots had a long way to go tonight. They dove down into gorges and followed them as long as they dared. They hugged cliff walls at every opportunity to decrease their radar profile. And they climbed.

That was the true danger—they would be up near the Black Hawks' limits when they crossed over the backbone of the Himalayas in their rush for India. The air was so rarefied that they burned fuel at a prodigious rate. Their reserve didn't allow for any extended battles while crossing the border…not for any battle at all really.

# # #

It was pitch dark outside her helicopter when Captain Danielle Delacroix stamped on the left rudder pedal while giving the Black Hawk right control on cyclic. It tipped her most of the way onto her side, but let her continue in a straight line. A Black Hawk's rotor was fifty-four feet across. By cross-controlling her bird to tip it, she managed to execute a straight line between two pylons only thirty feet apart.

At her current angle of attack, she took up less than a half-rotor of width, twenty-four feet. That left her three feet to either side, sufficient as she was moving at under a hundred knots.

The training instructor sitting beside her in the copilot's seat didn't react as she

swooped through the training course in
Fort Campbell, Kentucky.

After two years of training with the
U.S. Army's 160th Special Operations
Aviation Regiment, she was ready for some
action. At least she was convinced that she
was. But the trainers of Fort Campbell,
Kentucky had not signed off on her class
yet. Nor had they given any hint of when
they might.

She ducked under a bridge and bounced
into a near vertical climb to clear the power
line on the far side. Like a ride at *le carnaval,*
only with five thousand horsepower.

To even apply to SOAR required five
years of prior military rotorcraft experi-
ence. She had applied because of a chance
encounter—or rather what she'd thought
was a chance encounter at the time.

Captain Justin Roberts had been a top
Chinook pilot, the one who had convinced
her to cross-train from her beloved Black
Hawk and try out the massive twin-rotor
craft. He'd made the jump from the 10th
Mountain Division to the 160th SOAR
after he'd been in the service for five years.

Then one night she'd been having pizza in Watertown, New York a couple miles off the 10th's base at Fort Drum. Justin had greeted her with surprise and shared her pizza. Had said he was just in town visiting old haunts. Her questions had naturally led to discussions of his experiences at SOAR. He'd even paid for the pizza after eating half.

He'd left her interested enough to fill out an application to the 160th. The speed at which she was rushed into testing told her that her meeting with Justin hadn't been by chance and that she owed him more than half a pizza next time they met. She'd asked around once she'd passed the qualification exams and a brutal set of interviews that had left her questioning her sanity, never mind her ability. "Justin Roberts is presently deployed, ma'am," was the only response she'd ever gotten.

The training course was never the same, but it always had a time limit. The time would be short and they didn't tell you what it was. So she drove the Black Hawk for all it was worth like Regina Jaquess waterskiing her way to U.S. Ski Team female athlete of the year.

The Night Stalkers were a damned secretive lot, and after two years of training, she understood why. With seven years flying for the 10th, she'd thought she was good.

She'd been one of the top pilots at Fort Drum.

The Night Stalkers had offered an education in what it really meant to fly. In the two years of training, she'd flown more hours than in the seven years prior, despite two deployments to Iraq. And spent more time in the classroom than her life-to-date accumulated flight hours.

But she was ready now. It was *très viscérale,* right down in her bones she could feel it. The Black Hawk was as much a part of her nervous system as breathing. As were the Little Bird and the massive Chinook.

She dove down into a canyon and slid to a hover mere inches over the reservoir inside the thirty-second window laid out on the flight plan.

Danielle resisted a sigh. She was ready for something to happen and to happen soon.

# # #

Pete Napier and his two fellow Black Hawks crossed into the mountainous province of Sikkim, India ten feet over the glaciers and still moving fast. It was an hour before dawn.

"Twenty minutes of fuel remaining," Nicolai said it like personal challenge when they hit the border.

"Thanks, I never would have noticed."

It had been a nail-biting tradeoff: the more fuel he burned, the more easily he climbed due to the lighter load. The more he climbed, the faster he burned what little fuel remained.

He climbed hard as Nicolai counted down the minutes remaining, burning fuel even faster than he had been crossing the mountains of southern Tibet. They caught up with the U.S. Air Force HC-130P Combat King refueling tanker with only ten minutes of fuel left.

"Ram that bitch."

Pete extended the refueling probe which extended beyond the forward edge of the rotor blade and drove at the basket trailing behind the tanker on its long hose.

He nailed it on the first try despite the fluky winds.

"Ah," Nicolai sighed. "It is better than the sex," his thick Russian accent only ever surfaced in this moment or in a bar while picking up women.

His helo had the least fuel due to having the most men aboard, so he was first in line. His Number Two picked up the second refueling basket trailing off the other wing of the HC-130P. A quick five hundred gallons and he was breathing much more easily.

Another two hours of—thank god—straight and level flight at altitude, and they arrived at the aircraft carrier awaiting them in the Bay of Bengal. India had agreed to turn a blind eye as long as the Americans never actually touched their soil.

Once out on deck—and the worst of the kinks worked out—he pulled his team together, six pilots and six crew chiefs.

"Honor to serve!" He saluted them sharply.

"Hell yeah!" They shouted in response and saluted in turn. It their version of spiking the football in the end zone.

A petty officer in a bright green vest appeared at his elbow, "Follow me please, sir." He pointed toward the Navy-gray command structure that towered above the carrier's deck. The Commodore of the entire carrier group was waiting for him just outside the entrance.

The green escorted him across the hazards of the busy flight deck. Pete pulled his helmet on to buffer the noise of an F-18 Hornet firing up and being flung off the catapult.

"Orders, Major Napier," the Commodore handed him a folded sheet. "Hate to lose you."

The Commodore saluted, which Pete automatically returned before looking down at the sheet of paper in his hands. The man was gone before the import of Pete's orders slammed in.

A different green showed up with his duffle and began guiding him toward a loading C-2 Greyhound twin prop airplane. It was parked number two for the launch catapult, close behind the raised jet-blast deflector.

What in the name of fuck-all had he done to deserve this?

He glanced at the orders again as he stumbled up the Greyhound's rear ramp and crash landed into a seat.

Training rookies?

It was worse than a demotion.

This was punishment.

*****

Available at fine retailers everywhere

More information at:
www.mlbuchman.com

Other works by M.L. Buchman

The Night Stalkers
The Night Is Mine
I Own the Dawn
Daniel's Christmas
Wait Until Dark
Frank's Independence Day
Peter's Christmas
Take Over at Midnight
Light Up the Night
Bring On the Dusk

Firehawks
Pure Heat
Wildfire at Dawn
Full Blaze
Wildfire at Larch Creek
Wildfire on the Skagit
Hot Point

Angelo's Hearth
Where Dreams are Born
Where Dreams Reside
Maria's Christmas Table
Where Dreams Unfold
Where Dreams Are Written

Dieties Anonymous

Cookbook from Hell: Reheated
Saviors 101

Thrillers

Swap Out!
One Chef!
Two Chef!

SF/F Titles

Nara
Monk's Maze